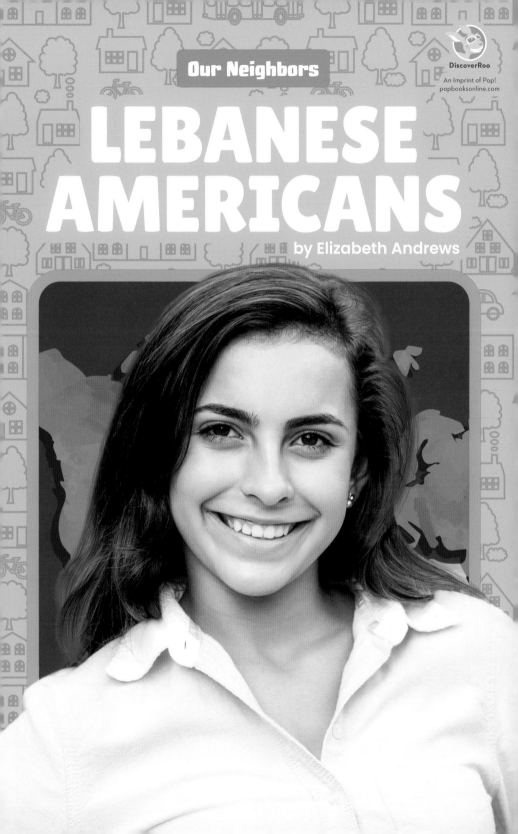

Our Neighbors

DiscoverRoo
An Imprint of Pop!
popbooksonline.com

LEBANESE
AMERICANS

by Elizabeth Andrews

abdobooks.com

Published by Pop!, a division of ABDO, PO Box 398166, Minneapolis, Minnesota 55439. Copyright ©2022 by Abdo Consulting Group, Inc. International copyrights reserved in all countries. No part of this book may be reproduced in any form without written permission from the publisher. DiscoverRoo™ is a trademark and logo of Pop!.

Printed in the United States of America, North Mankato, Minnesota.

052021
092021

 THIS BOOK CONTAINS RECYCLED MATERIALS

Cover Photos: Shutterstock images

Interior Photos: Shutterstock images, 1, 6, 9, 11, 14–15, 18, 26; iStockphoto, 5, 17, 21, 25, 29; Rihan/AP/Shutterstock, 13; Historia/Shutterstock, 22 (top and bottom); Eddie Tamerian/AP/Shutterstock, 23 (bottom); Steve Bent/ANL/Shutterstock, 23 (top left); NABIL MOUNZER/EPA-EFE/Shutterstock, 23 (top right)

Editor: Tyler Gieseke
Series Designer: Laura Graphenteen

Library of Congress Control Number: 2020948869

Publisher's Cataloging-in-Publication Data

Names: Andrews, Elizabeth, author.

Title: Lebanese Americans / by Elizabeth Andrews

Description: Minneapolis, Minnesota : Pop!, 2022 | Series: Our neighbors | Includes online resources and index.

Identifiers: ISBN 9781098240042 (lib. bdg.) | ISBN 9781644945988 (pbk.) | ISBN 9781098240967 (ebook)

Subjects: LCSH: Lebanese Americans--Juvenile literature. | Ethnicity--United States--Juvenile literature. | Neighbors--Juvenile literature. | Immigrants--United States--History--Juvenile literature.

Classification: DDC 973.004--dc23

WELCOME TO DiscoverRoo!

Pop open this book and you'll find QR codes loaded with information, so you can learn even more!

Scan this code* and others like it while you read, or visit the website below to make this book pop!

popbooksonline.com/lebanese-americans

*Scanning QR codes requires a web-enabled smart device with a QR code reader app and a camera.

TABLE OF CONTENTS

CHAPTER 1

FAMILY FESTIVITIES

Aida woke up to the smell of chopped parsley, onions, and mint drifting down the hall. She fell asleep to the sound of chopping vegetables the night before.

WATCH A VIDEO HERE!

The whole week had been busy. Her family was cleaning and preparing for her older brother's graduation party.

Older family members will pass down special recipes to their children.

After the bulgur wheat shell of the kibbeh is formed, it's filled with meat.

Aida's family enjoys throwing big

parties. From birthdays and holidays

to a good report card, celebrations are

always in order. The parties involve the

entire extended family.

Her family's kitchen was filled with

people. The aunts were busy forming

kibbeh and cutting up *baklava*. Her dad

and uncles prepared the *shawarma*

cone. They used the chicken they started

marinating yesterday.

DID YOU KNOW? Shawarma cones cook meat slowly. People shave off the cooked outside of the cone as it spins.

Aida could see her brother trying to help. Their mom quickly shooed him away. Today was about him. He had graduated with great grades and would be going to a good college. The family was very proud.

The kitchen craziness was something that Aida loved about her Lebanese American home. Things were never done on a small scale. And they were always done with love.

Lebanese meals are very colorful and full of flavors.

Lebanon has one of the longest human histories on Earth. People of many religious backgrounds have called it home. It is located in a very important part of the world.

LEARN MORE HERE!

MAP OF LEBANON

Mediterranean Sea

LEBANON

Beirut

SYRIA

Lebanon borders the beautiful Mediterranean Sea. The sparkling blue waters and mountain landscape make Lebanon a pretty country to explore.

ISRAEL

WHERE IN THE WORLD?

JORDAN

EGYPT

SAUDI ARABIA

Unfortunately, people of different backgrounds had long-lasting disagreements. These sometimes led to violence.

In the early 1900s, the Lebanese were facing food shortages and financial problems. People began leaving the country for safer and more stable places. From the late 1800s through 1930, the first large group of **immigrants** came to the United States.

More large groups left Lebanon between 1945 and 1989. They were

People who lived in Lebanon got used to a military presence.

escaping two wars. The Arab-Israeli War created **political** disagreements in the country. Then the Lebanese **Civil War** forced people out of their homes. During these conflicts people lost jobs. They struggled to care for their families.

The United States offered a safe place for the Lebanese. They would be able to get good jobs. Families would

There is a 2,000-year-old Roman temple in Baalbek dedicated to the god Jupiter.

have easy access to food. They were

looking for a better life. They believed

they could get it in America.

CHAPTER 3

A PASSIONATE COMMUNITY

Lebanese **immigrants** arrived to the United States in different waves over the past 250 years. When they arrived in the US, they often moved to places where

COMPLETE AN ACTIVITY HERE!

groups of Lebanese Americans already

lived. Finding a community makes living

in a new country easier.

Lebanese food often uses lots of garlic and lemon.

Michigan, California, Ohio, and Massachusetts have many Lebanese Americans. They can make big impacts where they live. Often Lebanese restaurants or bakeries become people's favorite places to eat and spend time. This is because Lebanese American families run them. They put their heart into their work. It mixes what they are **passionate** about—food and family.

DID YOU KNOW? A staple food for Lebanese Americans is grape leaves! They fill them with meat and rice.

Lebanese parents' passion for family shapes how they raise their children. They want their kids to have a better life than they would in Lebanon. Sometimes Lebanese parents are **stricter** than other American parents. They might put more pressure on getting good grades. They may expect their kids to spend their free time at home with the family. Lebanese American families are very loyal. They know they can count on one another.

Lebanese parents and children grow close when they spend time together.

LEBANESE IMMIGRATION TIMELINE

Vue de Beyrouth et jardin
de Rustein Pacha.

1920
Lebanon becomes its own country outside the Ottoman Empire.

1854
The first recordered **immigration** of Lebanese to the United States occurs.

1915-1918
FIRST WAVE
Lebanon goes through a famine. Large groups of people immigrate to the United States.

1944
Lebanon gains its independence from France.

1945-1989
SECOND WAVE

Another large wave of immigration from Lebanon to the United States occurs because of the wars.

1975-1990

Neighbors fight neighbors during the Lebanese **Civil War**. Most disagreements had to do with religion.

1945-1967

Arabs use Lebanon as a military base during the Arab–Israeli War.

2000s:

Life in Lebanon remains difficult. There is fighting, and the government does not take good care of its people.

CHAPTER 4

HAPPY AT HOME

Lebanese Americans spend a lot of time in their homes. Carrying on their **culture** in America is important to them. The older generation wants the children to understand Lebanese traditions.

LEARN MORE HERE!

Usually, family members speak two languages. Many parents and grandparents want kids to be able to speak and write in Arabic.

Grandparents love to share wisdom with their grandchildren.

Almost 150 million people speak Arabic.

Lebanese American children are

taught to be proud of the culture they

come from. They learn about their

heritage when they are young.

As kids, they are also learning and growing at school. There, they spend time with peers who are different from them. They have time to figure out what sports or activities they enjoy.

AN ANCIENT LANGUAGE

Arabic is a very old language. It is very different from English. It has its own alphabet with 28 letters. Unlike English, the letters are always pronounced the same. Punctuation is less important in Arabic. There is no difference between an upper- and lower-case letter. In Arabic you read right to left, which is the opposite of English. The letters always trail together like cursive.

Sometimes the continued time with family is difficult. Kids of Lebanese **immigrants** have to find a balance of their two cultures. In Lebanese culture, parents have a lot of say in what their kids do with their lives. They want to see them succeed. In American culture, kids are much more independent in planning for their future.

DID YOU KNOW?

Lebanese Americans introduce themselves with their first and last names. They can tell a lot about a family's history through last names.

Lebanese American children meet kids from all kinds of backgrounds at school.

At school, Lebanese American children can become their own people. And those people are a beautiful mix of Lebanese and American culture. They are special!

MAKING CONNECTIONS

TEXT-TO-SELF

Many Lebanese American children can speak two languages. Is that something you would want to do? What language would you choose?

TEXT-TO-TEXT

Have you read other books about immigrants in America? What do they have in common with this title? How are they different?

TEXT-TO-WORLD

Some religious groups argue with each other in Lebanon. Can you think of another place that deals with the same issue? How have they worked to solve the arguments?

civil war — a war between people from the same country.

culture — the arts, beliefs, and ways of life of a group of people.

heritage — something that one believes, thinks, or does that comes from one's family or background.

immigrate — to enter another country to live. A person who immigrates is an immigrant.

marinate — to soak in a flavorful sauce.

passionate — capable of or expressing strong feeling.

political — having to do with the government.

strict — following or demanding others follow rules in a rigid, exact manner.

INDEX

ONLINE RESOURCES
popbooksonline.com

Scan this code* and others like it while you read, or visit the website below to make this book pop!

popbooksonline.com/lebanese-americans

*Scanning QR codes requires a web-enabled smart device with a QR code reader app and a camera.